NEGATIVES ATTRACT

The fiendish fun continues at

www.screamstreet.co

This is a work of fiction. Names, characters, places and incidents either are the product of the author's imagination or, if real, used fictitiously. All statements, activities, stunts, descriptions, information and material of any other kind contained herein are included for entertainment purposes only and should not be relied on for accuracy or replicated as they may result in injury.

First published 2016 by Walker Entertainment
An imprint of Walker Books Ltd
87 Vauxhall Walk, London SE11 5HJ

2 4 6 8 10 9 7 5 3 1

Based on the Scream Street series of books by Tommy Donbavand

Based on the scripts "Lovestruck!" by Mark Huckerby and Nick Ostler and "Resus Rocks" by Giles Pilbrow

This book has been typeset in Bembo Educational

Printed and bound in Great Britain by Clays Ltd, St Ives plc

British Library Cataloguing in Publication Data: a catalogue record for this book is available from the British Library

ISBN 978-1-4063-6787-4
www.walker.co.uk

NEGATIVES ATTRACT

Tommy Donbavand

LUKE WATSON

With a troublesome taste for adventure, Luke is much like any other teenage boy – oh, except for the fact that he's also a werewolf. If he gets upset, stay well clear of him!

CLEO FARR

Cleo is a feisty teen mummy who's been in Scream Street for centuries. She's used that time to become an expert at martial arts, which comes in handy rather often.

RESUS NEGATIVE

Resus is the sarcastic son of two vampires. But he didn't get the vampire gene himself, so there's no drinking blood or turning into a bat for him – much to his disappointment.

LUELLA

A trainee witch, Luella has an unfortunate tendency to get spells wrong – with disastrous results. She also has a tendency to freak out whenever her crush, Resus, is around.

EEFA

Luella's aunt is the proprietor of Eefa's Emporium, Scream Street's neighbourhood store. Thanks to a glamour spell, no one can see the fact that Eefa is really a 300-year-old witch.

DREAD

Brain Drain, a top flesh metal band, has gained a large following in Scream Street – and not just among zombies. Dread, the guitarist, isn't very nice, often treating his fans with disdain.

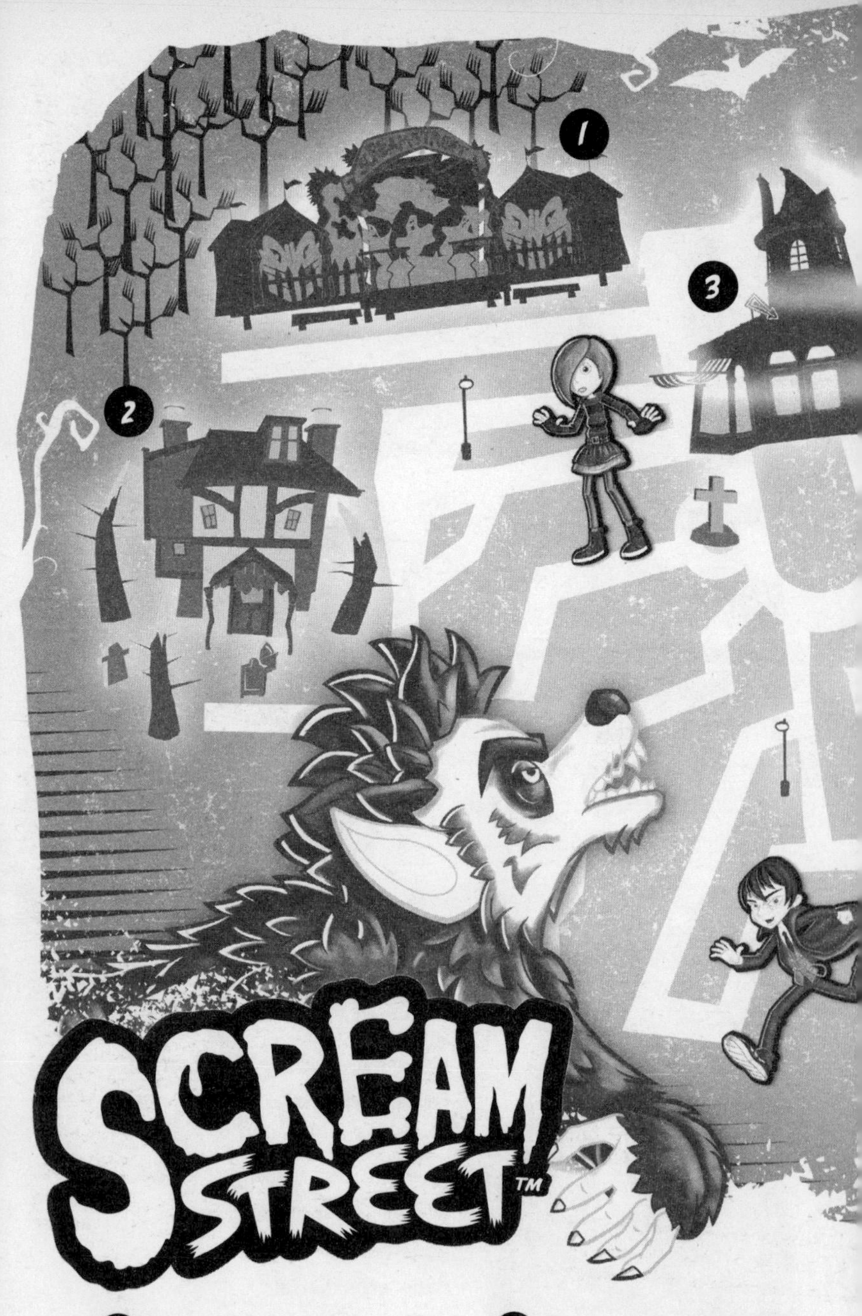

1 THE GHOST TRAIN

2 HAUNTED HOUSE

3 EEFA'S EMPORIUM

4 SNEER HALL

WHERE BEING A FREAK IS TOTALLY NORMAL...

5 CLEO'S HOUSE

6 THE GRAVEYARD

7 RESUS'S AND LUKE'S HOUSES

CONTENTS

Lovestruck

Chapter One: The Argument.................. 13

Chapter Two: The Spell.......................... 24

Chapter Three: The Blackmail............ 34

Chapter Four: The Jelly......................... 44

Chapter Five: The Battle....................... 54

Resus Rocks

Chapter One: The Game......................... 69

Chapter Two: The Band......................... 79

Chapter Three: The Replacement.... 88

Chapter Four: The Ego.......................... 98

Chapter Five: The Fog......................... 108

Excerpt from *UNINVITED GUESTS*..... 121

LOVESTRUCK

Chapter One

THE ARGUMENT

The room was the colour of blood. Red walls, red ceiling, red floor. Chairs with red covers surrounded a table covered with a scarlet cloth, and red curtains shielded the room from the harsh sunlight that would otherwise glare through the windows. Orangey-red flames flickered in a fireplace fronted by two enormous fangs, above which an ogre's head was mounted on a wooden plinth.

This was a house of vampires.

And yet, despite the well-accepted truth that vampires do not have reflections, a mirror hung on the wall. A mirror displaying the reflection of a young vampire. In one hand he clutched a hairbrush, and in the other a set of false fangs.

Resus Negative slipped the pointed dentures over his own front teeth and finished brushing his hair. Life as a normal child born into a long-established vampire family could be tough at times. Resus was naturally blond, with healthy pink skin, something he was forced to disguise with black hair dye and pale face paint. He couldn't speed-blur like vampires could, or turn into a bat. And the thought of drinking blood made his stomach churn.

But having a reflection was one of the few bonuses. His parents spent hours trying to tame their hairstyles. His mum frequently left the house with her face covered in make-up that would have been more at home daubed onto a clown. And the yelps of pain coming from the bathroom each morning suggested that his dad frequently had trouble shaving.

Resus had none of these problems. Mirrors were his friends – especially when there was no one around to watch him.

"Tonight on *Creature Talk*, we meet rock star and vampire legend Resus Negative!" he announced into the end of his hairbrush. Then he paused to imitate the roar of a large audience.

"So, what's it like being a vampire?" he asked himself.

Turning to his left, Resus replied in the distinctive accent of his distant Transylvanian relatives: "Vell, it's a pain in the neck! Ha, ha, ha! Only kidding, I love it! Anyvay, it's been great talking to you, but now I hev got to fly."

He spun on the spot, just the way his dad did when he was about to transform into a bat. But instead of sprouting wings, Resus got dizzy. He shot out a foot to steady himself, but caught it in the end of his cloak and crashed to the floor. His fake fangs went flying, and the stiff bristles of the hairbrush embedded themselves into his wrist.

"Ow!" he groaned, pulling the brush away and examining the damage. "That's gonna sting later!" He scurried across the floor on all fours to retrieve his dentures from where they'd slid beneath the couch.

As he reached under the settee, his mum's

voice rang out, and she didn't sound happy. "You never listen to me!"

A second, equally angry, voice replied. "What did you just say?"

Jumping to his feet, Resus clipped his fangs back in place and crept out into the corridor. His parents were in the kitchen and, as usual, they were having a row.

"Hand me that wrench!" insisted Alston Negative.

"Why should I?" demanded his wife, Bella. "What did your last servant die of?"

"A stake through the heart, if you must know!" replied Alston. "Oh, I'll get it myself!"

The vampire blurred across the kitchen, snatched a large wrench from his toolbox, and whizzed back to the sink. He began to adjust a bolt on the side of a brass tap that was shaped like a bat in flight.

"Admit it, you have no idea what you're doing," snapped Bella.

"Of course I do!" Alston retorted. "I think I can change a simple washer on the blood tap without having to call a plumber!"

"I doubt it," huffed Bella. "The last time you

tried DIY, you opened a portal to the Underlands in the bathroom!"

"I got rid of it again, didn't I?"

"Yes, but not before it had swallowed up all of my best towels!"

"Well, this time it will be different. All I have to do is—"

Suddenly, a fountain of glistening red blood spurted high into the air, splashing off the kitchen ceiling and spraying the entire room in a fine, crimson mist.

"Now look what you've done!" cried Bella.

"It wasn't my fault!" protested Alston. "You distracted me!"

"Oh, so it's all *my* fault, is it?"

"I didn't say that!"

In the hallway, Resus sighed. He took one last look at the blood raining down over his furious parents, then made for the front door.

Mr Crudley slithered across the well-trodden carpet of Eefa's Emporium, leaving a trail of sticky green slime in his wake. Tiny two-tailed tadpoles danced and swam in the river of rancid residue the bog monster left behind. Not that Mr Crudley cared – he had other matters on his mind.

Or, rather, he had other matters up his nostrils. He could smell something. Something sweet and succulent. He sniffed at the air, following the scent as keenly as a hungry werewolf tracking down its next victim.

The emporium was owned and run by a 300-year-old witch by the name of Eefa Everwell. None of her customers would have been able to guess the proprietor's true age; she wore an enchantment charm that hid her warty, wrinkled appearance beneath a vision of sheer beauty. Her looks often made people completely forget why they had visited the shop in the first place. And sometimes where they lived, as well.

Today, Eefa was in the stockroom, checking through her latest delivery of magic spells, potions, crystal balls and other paranormal paraphernalia. Keeping an eye on the shop was her niece and witch in training, Luella Everwell. The young witch was slumped against the counter, sighing heavily at being made to mind the till when there were better ways she could be passing the time – like lying on her bed and flicking through the latest edition of *Teen Witch* magazine.

Luella spotted Mr Crudley approaching and did her best to look attentive while not staring at the startling pattern of his baggy Hawaiian shirt. She needed to distract her senses from the garment, and her eyes fell on a plate loaded with cubes of jelly. That would have to do!

"Fancy trying one of our new jellies, Mr Crudley?" she asked. The bog monster slithered to a halt, skidding slightly in his own juices.

"Thank you, Luella!" Mr Crudley gurgled wetly. "Don't mind if I do! I thought I could smell something a little out of the ordinary."

Luella held out the platter of wobbly treats and Mr Crudley took it in his tendril-coated, webbed fingers, eyeing the colourful cubes hungrily.

"Now, which shall I try?" he asked himself. "Eeny, meeny, miney…"

Then he opened his cavernous mouth and swallowed all the jelly samples whole. And the tray as well. Wiping his rubbery lips, the bog monster belched loudly.

"Burp!"

Luella quickly turned away as a gust of rotten breath blew across her face.

"Oops!" Mr Crudley chuckled. "Pardon me!

Do you think I could sample a few more?"

But Luella was no longer listening. While avoiding the gruesome burp gas, she had spotted three new customers entering the store: boy werewolf Luke Watson, Egyptian mummy Cleo Farr and the dashing dreamboat that was Resus Negative.

Cleo led the way between the shelves to the First Aid department, where she dropped to her knees and began to sift through a basket of miscellaneous medical items, including tentacle treatments, talon repair kits and single contact lenses made especially for cyclopes.

"My parents are really at each other's throats lately," moaned Resus.

Luke shrugged. "They're vampires, Resus. That's what vampires do."

"Aha!" cried Cleo, pulling a package of bandages from a rack. "I really don't know why Eefa insists on keeping these in the First Aid section. They should be in Clothing."

Resus sighed. "Maybe my mum and dad are falling out of love."

"Don't worry," said Luke. "Parents argue all the time. I'm sure that, deep down, they love each other."

"Yeah," agreed Cleo. "Like, really deep down – below the heart, past the liver. Right down there in the bowels somewhere!"

Resus forced a smile as Cleo and Luke sauntered off to continue their shopping. He turned to follow— and jumped with fright. Luella was standing just centimetres away, staring up at him.

"Oh, hi Luella!" he said. "Gave me a fright there!"

"OMG, he said 'hi' to me!" hissed Luella to herself. "Keep it together. Focus. Deep breath!"

"Did you want something?" Resus asked, his eyes darting around as he tried to locate his friends.

"Um, yeah," said Luella. "It's just that I heard what you were saying about your mum and dad arguing. I mean, I wasn't eavesdropping or following you around the shop or staring at you from behind the spell books or anything like that!"

"Oh, I er..."

"Anyway, I was thinking that – being a witch and everything – I could, like, make a love spell for us."

Resus blinked. "Us?"

"*Them!*" exclaimed Luella quickly. "Totally

them! Your parents. I mean, only if you want. Maybe? No, forget it. I already have. I'm going to go now."

Resus took hold of Luella's arm as she made to leave. "You'd do that for me?"

Luella gazed up into the depths of Resus's eyes. "I'd do anything for you," she crooned. "Meet me at your house in half an hour, my dark angel!"

Then she dashed off in the direction of the shop counter and disappeared, leaving Resus feeling a little bewildered.

"O ... K."

Suddenly, Luella was back at his side. "I didn't mean anything by the 'dark angel' stuff," she assured him. "I call everyone that now. It's, like, my thing."

There was a damp, slurping noise as Mr Crudley slithered past on his way to the exit, stuffing another handful of jelly samples into his enormous mouth. "Delicious jellies, Luella!" he proclaimed, before burping loudly again. "Whoops!"

"Thanks, Mr Crudley!" said Luella. She glanced up at Resus's confused expression and added, "My dark angel!"

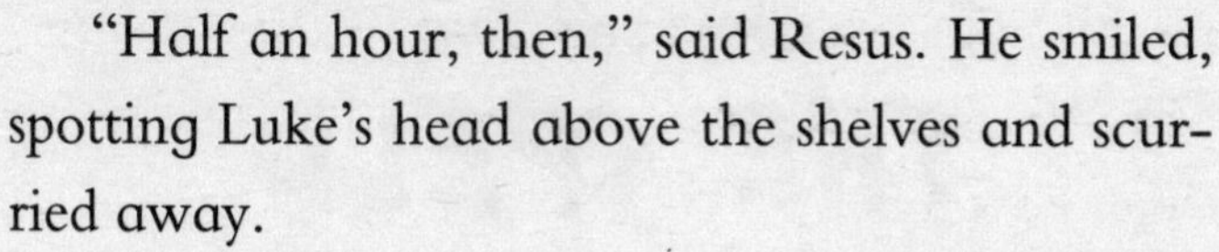
"Half an hour, then," said Resus. He smiled, spotting Luke's head above the shelves and scurried away.

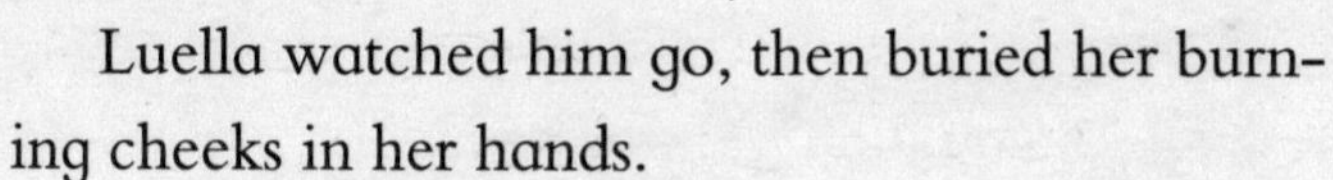
Luella watched him go, then buried her burning cheeks in her hands.

Chapter Two

THE SPELL

Eefa Everwell waved her hand in the air, and a floating pencil ticked off items on the long list left by the recently departed delivery driver.

Carbonated bile for Scream Street's zombies? Tick!

Copies of the latest book by children's horror author MT Graves? Tick!

Sachets of lightly dusted scabs – the perfect treat for any paranormal pet? Tick!

Two boxes of jelly cubes… Wait a minute!

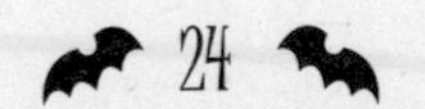

The witch snatched her pencil from the air and hurried over towards a huge stack of identical cardboard containers. The delivery company hadn't just brought two boxes of jelly. Instead, she had *twenty-two* of them!

Eefa was just about to put a curse on her supplier when Luella dashed in.

"Auntie Eefa!" she cried. "Could you teach me how to make a love potion?"

Eefa placed her hands on her hips and stared down at her trainee. "And why would you need one of those?"

"It's, er, for a school project," Luella lied.

"Hasn't Dr Skully banned the use of magic in the classroom ever since you cast a spell on your trombone to cheat on your music exam?" Eefa scowled.

"Er, yes!" said Luella. "And that's precisely why he wants me to learn how to make one at home."

"Well, all right," said Eefa cautiously. She crossed over to a table stacked with spell ingredients and began to gather some of them into a mixing bowl. "But do try to pay attention this time."

"Of course!" beamed Luella.

"Now, your common or garden love spell is equal parts rose petals, milk chocolate, jellyfish and cherub spittle."

Luella pulled a disgusted face. "Cherub spittle?"

Eefa nodded. "Cherub tears work, but cherub spittle is better." The witch tipped her mixture into a mortar and used a pestle to grind the ingredients together. A few seconds later, the concoction began to glow and smoke.

"Is that it?" asked Luella.

"That's it!" confirmed Eefa, holding up her palm. The smoke formed a shimmering heart-tipped arrow just above her hand. "Hey presto, you're ready to get loved up!"

She led Luella to the stockroom door and swung it open. Outside, they found Resus's pet leech, Lulu, snuffling around the dustbins. Eefa took careful aim, and threw the tiny red arrow directly at the creature. Lulu shuddered as her body absorbed the potent potion.

"Now, watch carefully," whispered Eefa to her niece. "Lulu should fall in love with the next creature she sees."

"Yip!"

Eefa and Luella jumped as Dig the dog bounded round the corner, his fur-covered nose sniffing at the air and skeletal back legs skidding on the damp tarmac.

Lulu took one look at the half-dog and flushed a deeper red. Slithering forward, she planted a wet, slimy kiss right on the partial pooch's snout.

Dig's eyes snapped wide open and, with a terrified *yelp*, he raced off, an obsessed Lulu slowly squelching after him.

"Ugh," groaned Eefa as she slammed the stockroom door. "That's put me right off my dinner!"

Luella hurried over to the table and grabbed the rest of the glowing love spell. "Thanks, Auntie Eefa!" she beamed. "This is exactly what I need!"

"I don't think so!" said Eefa, snatching the potion from Luella's grasp. She opened the door to the furnace and tossed the spell inside, where it exploded in a spectacular shower of scarlet sparks.

"But I promised!"

"It's against the witch's code to allow a trainee to use a love spell, and well you know

it!" Eefa reminded her. "They're far too powerful, and potentially dangerous."

Before Luella could argue any further, a gargled cry came from the shop floor. "Hello?" called Mr Crudley. "Jelly! I need more jelly!"

Eefa sighed and grabbed one of the many boxes of the stuff from the pile near the door. "Coming Mr Crudley!" she cried, before adding to herself, "Maybe I will be able to sell all twenty-two boxes after all."

Luella leaned back against Eefa's work table and sulked. Eefa never trusted her with anything more than the most basic of spells. How was she supposed to learn if she wasn't given the chance to practise?

"I mean, how hard could it be?" she muttered to herself. "I've just watched her mix a batch of the stuff, and it didn't seem at all dangerous. I bet I could make a love potion in under a minute."

A smile spread across her face as the idea formed. Keeping one eye on the door to the shop, she quickly grabbed the same spell ingredients she remembered her aunt using and dropped them into the bowl.

"Rose petals," she said to herself as she

worked. "Cherub spittle – yuck! Milk chocolate and ... and... Oh, what was it?"

Another great *burp!* resounded from the shop floor, and Luella's eye fell on the stack of recently delivered boxes. "That's it!" she exclaimed. "Jelly!"

Resus sat on the edge of the flower bed beneath the living-room window and listened to his mum rant about one thing after another: how many repairs the house needed, why it was always she who had to feed the local wild scorpions, and how there was no way they could afford yet another rise in the rent.

The vampire buried his face in his hands and sighed. Were his parents going for a world record in arguing? He hadn't heard his mum shout so much since the day he'd accidentally mixed up her coffin freshener spray with a can of instant spider eggs.

"Hello!"

Startled, Resus looked up to see Luella standing near the garden gate, gazing dreamily at him. "Oh, hi Luella," he said, climbing to his feet and heading over to join her.

The trainee witch said nothing. She simply stared, unblinking. Resus clicked his fingers in front of her face, and she jerked back to reality.

"Oh, right. Hi! I've, um … got the spell."

She opened her hand to reveal a glowing arrow floating just above her palm. However, unlike the bright crimson colour of Eefa's creation, this one was more of a vibrant pink.

"Wow!" said Resus, impressed. "Did you make that all by yourself?"

"It's no big deal," said Luella, trying hard not to blush. "It's just a common or garden love spell, you know. It makes the target fall in love with the first person they see."

"That sounds perfect!" said Resus.

"So, like, er, where are your folks?" Luella asked.

Resus jabbed a thumb over his shoulder. "Inside, arguing as usual."

"Then we've no time to lose!" said Luella, grabbing Resus's hand and leading him back to his spot beneath the window. "OMG!" she hissed to herself. "Holding hands! Holding hands!"

"I've already told you!" bellowed Bella Negative from inside the house. "We just can't afford a rent rise like that!"

Resus and Luella ducked beneath the window together. "Are you sure this is going to work?" the vampire asked in a whisper.

"Do witches ride brooms?" Luella replied.

There was a slight pause. "Actually, I'm not really sure," Resus admitted. "I mean, I've *heard* about witches riding broomsticks, but I've never seen it for myself."

"Neither have I," said Luella. "I asked Eefa if I could have one for my birthday, but she said no, as usual! She's, like, so mean!"

"Don't you dare take that tone with me!" hollered Bella from the living room, her shadow falling on the closed curtains.

"Quickly!" urged Resus. "Now!"

"What? Oh, yes! The love potion!" Taking aim, Luella hurled the love spell at the shadow. It twinkled as it passed through the windowpane, before erupting in a cascade of pink sparks all around Mrs Negative's silhouette.

When Bella next spoke, she no longer sounded angry. In fact, her voice was dripping with unbridled love. "Come here, you big beautiful man!"

Resus grinned widely, and high-fived Luella.

"It worked! Thanks!"

Luella sighed happily. "Anything for you, my dark—"

"Hey, kids! Having fun?"

Resus and Luella spun round at the voice. Alston Negative was walking up the path towards the front door, a freshly purchased newspaper tucked beneath his arm.

"Oh, no," said Luella.

"Dad!" cried Resus. "If you're out here, who's in there with Mum?"

Crash!

The front door to 11 Scream Street slammed open and the terrified figure of Mayor Sir Otto Sneer came tumbling out. "Waaaaah!" he cried, racing for the gate and knocking Alston to the ground in the process. "Get her away from me!"

Then Bella appeared, leaping over her horizontal husband and giving chase, eyelids fluttering as she fixed her gaze on the new love of her life. "Come back, my lovely lump of love!"

Resus and Luella exchanged a worried glance, then they also jumped over Alston and hurried away after the unsuited sweethearts.

"Bye Dad!"

Alston lay on the path for a few more seconds until he was certain no one else was about to hurtle over him. Then he sat up, confused.

"Would somebody like to tell me what's going on?" he asked.

Chapter Three

THE BLACKMAIL

"Otto and Bella, sitting in a coffin, K-I-S-S-I-N-G!" sang Bella as she danced through the woods on the outskirts of Scream Street.

Oh, why had she never seen the mayor like this before? In all the years she had known him and his penny-pinching, self-serving schemes, she had believed him to be a selfish, cruel little man with bad breath and hairy knuckles. But now, somehow, her eyes had been opened.

She paused to rest against a tree. She pictured

herself hand in hand with her newfound love, walking up the wedding aisle together as her now ex-husband, Alston, stood by, sobbing.

Well, it was his own fault for not being like her precious Otto – short, overweight and almost completely bald.

Smiling happily, Bella raised a long, red-painted nail and scratched their initials into the bark of the tree: "BN + OS 4 eva!" She sighed as she carved a heart shape to surround the initials. Taking a step back, she studied her work, wondering how long the inscription would last, and how many future generations would pass by and know of the true love she felt for Otto Sneer.

It turned out to be not that long.

"Oi!" barked the tree, slapping her hand away with the flick of a branch and rubbing away her handiwork. "Go and scratch someone else!"

But a scolding from a talking tree wasn't enough to dampen Bella's mood. She skipped happily away, picturing the most beautiful black wedding dress she'd ever seen.

The woods were silent for a few moments, then Otto Sneer stepped out from within a particularly dense bush and breathed a heavy sigh of relief. "Thank goodness she's gone!" he muttered to himself. "I always knew vampires were a little on the crazy side, but she takes the biscuit. She's off her rocker! What in the name of all things freaky has come over her?"

A twig snapped. Otto leapt back into the bush to hide, terrified that Bella was returning, probably with a bouquet of poisonous plants and fearsome flowers. But it was just her son, Resus, and that girl from the emporium. They appeared to be searching the woods for someone. Probably his mad mother.

He was about to step out and confront them, when he spotted something in the young witch's hand. No, not *in* her hand, but hovering a few centimetres above it. A small, shimmering pink arrow. A *love spell*!

Otto grinned. So, *that's* what had happened to Bella. That's why she'd suddenly declared her undying love for him. She'd been hit by a stray spell. Of course, he'd known something was amiss when she'd tried to kiss him halfway through a discussion about rent rises. That wasn't usually how residents reacted to being forced into paying more for their crummy little homes.

As Resus and Luella hurried past, Otto stayed hidden and began to hatch a plan.

Hours later, Resus paced back and forth on top of one of the largest tombs in Scream Street's graveyard. Luella slumped against a nearby gravestone, bathed in the light of the full moon above.

"Well, I don't know where she's gone," groaned Resus. "We've searched everywhere!"

Luella nodded in agreement. "Like, more than everywhere!"

"And it's all our fault!" Resus wailed. "We made my mum fall in love with Otto!"

"Yeah," said Luella. "I feel, like, totally bad about that."

An idea occurred to Resus, and he stopped pacing. "It might wear off," he said, a hint of optimism creeping into his voice. "It might just be a temporary thing! How long do love spells last?"

"Um..." said Luella, thinking hard. "I'm not sure, but I think it's, like, for ever."

"What?" cried Resus, dropping to his knees. "This can't be happening."

"I know," said Luella. "I'm so sorry, Resus. I was only trying to help!"

"It's OK," Resus said with a sigh. "I know you were. I guess we're in this together."

Luella climbed on top of the tomb in a flash. She knelt before Resus, staring deep into his eyes. "We're together?" she gasped. "OMG, we totally are! It's like we're on the run or something. Oh, that's so romantic!"

"Yes," cackled a gruff voice from nearby. "Oh, so romantic!"

Otto's face suddenly appeared between Resus and Luella. The pair jumped with fright and tumbled off the top of the tomb.

"Whoa!" yelled Resus.

Otto strode back and forth on top of the tomb, a wicked smile pasted across his pallid features. "I do apologize for breaking up your little tête-à-tête like this. It looked as though you were getting *very* friendly."

"Yes, we so were!" sighed Luella.

Resus blinked in her direction. "Were we?"

Luella opened her mouth to reply, but Otto spoke first. "It doesn't matter, either way. You see, I know what's been going on here."

"You do?" questioned Resus.

"I most certainly do," Otto snarled. "We have

an apprentice witch using a love spell!"

Luella's cheeks paled in the moonlight. "Oh, dear."

"Oh, dear, indeed!" cackled Otto, continuing to pace. "Tut, tut, my dear. Using a love spell whilst still a trainee is very much against the witch's code, unless I'm mistaken – and I rarely am! This is a *very* juicy piece of information!"

The mayor turned to leave.

Luella clasped her hands together. "Please don't tell my aunt!" she begged. "I'll be grounded for, like, all eternity!"

Otto paused and turned. "I suppose I could keep it a secret," he said. "But you'd have to do something for me."

"Anything!" said Luella, her eyes wide with fear.

The mayor resumed his pacing. "You see, what happened today was not an unusual occurrence in my life. People fall in love with me all the time."

"Yeah, right!" muttered Resus.

"But then," Otto continued, "not everyone is as blessed as myself in the looks department! And those sad, ugly people, most of them living in the

normal world, could really use a love spell to help them overcome their many flaws and attract a mate. A love spell available exclusively from me, for a handsome price!"

Luella gasped. "You can't mean…"

"I most certainly do!" sneered Otto. "Mix me a big batch of love potion by morning, and Eefa need never know what you and your shampire friend here have been up to."

"O… OK!" said Luella, blinking back tears. "I'll do it."

"Well, hurry along then!" Otto snapped. "Time is money!"

With a final lingering look back at Resus, Luella got to her feet and trudged out of the graveyard in the direction of Eefa's Emporium.

The vampire turned back to glare up at the mayor, who was rubbing his hands together with glee. "You're despicable!" he hissed.

"Yeah, well, you're a fake-fanged fool," Otto retorted. "Just make sure you keep your maniac mother away from me!"

Then the mayor leapt down from the top of the tomb and disappeared into the night.

Resus slumped back against the nearest

headstone and stared up at the full moon. "Oh, Mum," he said to no one in particular. "Where are you?"

Bella Negative had been waiting outside Sneer Hall all night, clutching a bunch of dead flowers and composing love poems about her darling Otto. The mayor had managed to avoid her by slipping in through a side door when he got home from his business in the graveyard.

By dawn the following day, a crowd had gathered to watch as Bella tossed flowers over the front gates of Sneer Hall, chanting her lamentable lines of love.

"You might be really stinky,
With breath as stale as can be,
But, Otto Sneer, my baby.
You're the only one for me!"

Near the back of the audience, Resus pulled his cloak up to cover his face. Luke and Cleo shared a worried look.

"When you told us what happened yesterday, I didn't really believe you," said Luke. "But now

I'm seeing it with my own eyes."

"It's like watching a crash at the chariot races back in Egypt," added Cleo. "You know you shouldn't be watching, but you just can't tear your eyes away from the carnage!"

At the gates, Bella continued her romantic recital.

"You big, bald man,
With hairy knees,
Let me hold you tight,
My darling, please!"

"This is *so* wrong!" Resus moaned.

Luke's eyes widened as he stared through the crowd. "I think it's just gone even wronger!" he gasped.

"That's not a real word," said Cleo.

"Maybe not," said Luke. "But it's the only way I could think of to describe *that*."

Cleo followed his gaze. "Oh, my goodness!" she cried.

The crowd had fallen silent in astonishment as Bella completed her poem.

"Just one look at,
Your gorgeous belly,
Makes my legs,
Turn to—"

Awoblobloblob!

In front of everyone in Scream Street, Resus's mum had shivered, shaken and then collapsed to the ground, where she had transformed into a quivering mound of scarlet jelly, complete with eyes and mouth.

Chapter Four

THE JELLY

Luella dashed from shelf to shelf, grabbing handfuls of spell ingredients and dumping them into one of Eefa's huge cauldrons.

"Rose petals, milk chocolate, cherub spittle, jelly!" she said to herself over and over as the concoction took shape. "Now, mix together well."

Grabbing a long-handled wooden spoon, she began to stir the potion. Gradually, it began to glow a familiar shade of pink.

"Step away from the cauldron!" barked a voice.

Luella spun around to see Luke, Resus and Cleo in the doorway of the stockroom.

"I can't!" she cried. "If I don't have this ready soon, Otto's going to tell my aunt what I've been doing!"

"It's OK," said Resus. "Mayor Otto stopped us outside. He said the deal is off; he doesn't want your love potion any more."

"Yay!" cried Luella.

"Mainly because it has turned Mrs Negative into a big blob of wobbly jelly," Luke added.

"Not yay!" said Luella, her eyes flicking around the room. She looked from the boxes of jelly cubes to the jar of jellyfish sitting on the shelf above the cauldron.

"OMG! Jelly*fish*! It was meant to be jellyfish! I've got to destroy this stuff before it can do any more harm!"

Resus grabbed one side of the cauldron and helped Luella carry it towards the open door of the freshly stoked furnace.

Cleo darted forward. "Hold on!" she exclaimed. "You've got a powerful love spell that turns people to jelly, and you're about to set it on fire! Luella, are you sure this is a good idea?"

"I'm not sure of anything any more," Luella moaned. "I just want to forget this ever happened. Resus, please help me!"

Together the witch and the vampire emptied the contents of the cauldron over the red-hot flames of the furnace, and …

… absolutely nothing happened at all.

For a few seconds.

Then the furnace began to rumble.

"Uh oh!" said Luella.

The flames inside began to flicker pink.

"Oh, dear," said Resus.

The entire emporium started to shake.

"This isn't good!" Cleo and Luke clung to each other, eyes screwed closed.

Kaboom!

Hundreds of pink arrows exploded upwards from the inferno, escaped through the chimney above the shop, and rained down on the residents of Scream Street.

"Quick!" cried Luke. "Outside!"

Racing into the street, the kids skidded to a halt in horror at the chaos that confronted them.

Mrs Crudley was the first to receive a direct hit from one of the love arrows. She turned to her

nearest unsuspecting neighbour – Doug the zombie – and slithered sensuously in his direction.

"Whoa, big bog lady!" Doug yelled, making a dash for the graveyard. "This is most definitely not cool! We're barely on speaking terms!"

But Mrs Crudley wasn't giving up without a fight. She pursued the creeped-out corpse between the headstones, lips pursed and ready to kiss.

Desperate to escape, Doug began to disassemble himself – ripping off body parts and hurling them into the distance. Eventually, there was nothing left but a horrified head. Mrs Crudley snatched him up and began to cover him with slimy kisses.

"Not cool at all!" Doug wailed, when he could finally come up for air.

Back outside the emporium, Eefa was next to be pierced by a love arrow. She swayed on the spot slightly, then turned to gaze adoringly at NoName, Otto Sneer's blank-faced henchman. As the witch ran towards him, arms outstretched, the giant bodyguard turned to flee, only to collide with a lamp post and collapse to the ground.

Eefa was on him in a second, cuddling him as

if he were an enormous teddy bear. "Oh, he's so cute!" she squealed. "I wish my arms were longer so they could reach all the way around him."

Luke's mum, Sue Watson, was happily plucking weeds from her flower bed when Farp, one of Scream Street's resident goblins, was hit by a wayward arrow. He stopped and stared through the wooden slats of the fence at his new love interest.

"Oh, hello," said Sue, not quite sure what was happening. "Is there anything I can do for you?"

Farp took a deep breath, gritted his teeth, and then – *blatt!* – farted out a great stinking burst of green gas in the shape of a heart.

While his wife was busy cradling Doug's head in her vast arms and covering the corpse's cranium with kisses, Mr Crudley had finally found a nice quiet place to sit and eat his breakfast. The wooden slats of a bench just off the central square creaked and groaned as he lowered himself into position.

He pulled a flowered tablecloth from his pocket and tucked it into the neck of his shirt. Then, licking his lips, he opened up a large paper bag. Inside, glistening in the morning light, were hundreds of cubes of succulent, sugary jelly.

"Jelly!" he exclaimed, drooling, just as a pearlescent pink projectile zipped around the corner and caught him right between the eyes.

The bog monster blinked, belched, and then beheld his breakfast in a brand new light. This was no longer just a fantastic feast of trembling treats – it was the most beautiful collection of quivering cubes Mr Crudley had ever set his bulging eyes upon.

"*Jelly!*" he roared, before snatching up handfuls of the gelatine goodies and stuffing them into his huge mouth.

Luke ducked a passing potion arrow and risked a glance up at the chimney above Eefa's Emporium. "I think they're slowing down!" he said to the others. "We might be past the worst."

As he finished speaking, Doug's half-dog, Dig, galloped past, still trying to escape from Resus's pet, Lulu. She, in turn, was being hotly pursued by Scream Street's skeletal schoolteacher, Dr Skully.

"Ooh, I've never felt this way about a leech before!" the bony professor cried. "Come here and let me whisper sweet nothings into whatever you've got for ears!"

"I'm not entirely certain I agree with you," Cleo commented to Luke.

On the other side of the street, the mayor's assistant, Dixon, was trying in vain to hug a particularly piqued poltergeist. "Argue with me all you like, but I know you feel the same way as I do," the lovestruck teenager declared. "I can see right through you!"

But every time he managed to wrap his arms around the grumpy ghost, it let loose a fizzing burst of energy that sent its suitor flying through the air.

Luke winced as Dixon landed with a *splash* in a garden pond three houses away. The apprentice clambered to his feet, dozens of hungry piranhas chomping on his jacket and lank, green hair. "You've got such spirit!" he announced, heading back for another hug.

Resus spun to face Luella. "You have to do something!" he said urgently. "You have to fix this mess!"

"I don't know how!" Luella protested.

"Maybe not," said Resus. "But you know someone who does."

Luella looked over Resus's shoulder to where

her aunt, Eefa, was trying to dance the tango with a terrified NoName.

"No!" she wailed. "I can't tell Eefa what I did! She'll be furious!"

Cleo's dad, Niles Farr, careered around the corner, chasing after the bat that usually hung above the doorway to the emporium. "Come here, gorgeous!" he bellowed.

Resus kept his gaze fixed on Luella. "We're both in this together, remember? And we'll take our punishment together when everything gets back to normal. But right now, it's up to you!"

Luella nodded and, jumping out of the way as Dixon crashed, giggling, into the dustbins outside the emporium, she hurried across the street to try to get through to her entranced aunt.

"Aunt Eefa!" she shouted. "Look at me! Please!"

But the older witch was too giddy with desire to pay her niece the slightest bit of notice. "Look at his beautiful face!" Eefa sighed, running her fingers over NoName's flat features. "He's so handsome! I just love him!"

"No, you don't!" Luella protested. "It's just a spell! This is all my fault. I tried to copy your love

spell and I messed up! How do I stop it? Please, Eefa, tell me!"

Eefa's eyes flickered for a second, then she battled her way out from beneath the potion's power. She scanned the street before scowling down at her young apprentice.

"You did what?"

"I know!" Luella yelled. "I'm, like, really sorry! Quickly, tell me how to fix this!"

Eefa swayed as the love spell began to regain control. "You … must use … an emer-emergency U.U.S," she croaked. "Be sure … to… Flobalobalobalob!"

Luella watched in shock as her aunt fell with a *splat* to the pavement, now a big blob of jelly with eyes and a mouth, just like Bella Negative.

Splat! Splat! Splat!

All around Scream Street, the victims of the love spell were transforming into multicoloured mounds of jiggling jelly.

"Thank goodness for that!" gasped Sue Watson, as the gaseous goblin chasing her became little more than a dollop of dessert.

"Looks like we've got ourselves a bit of breathing space," said Luke. "Now, Luella, what did your aunt say? What's a U.U.S.?"

Before Luella could reply, a sickeningly wet, squelchy sound filled the air. Luke, Resus and Cleo turned to see Mr Crudley slide into view. They held onto each other as the bog monster threw back his bulbous head and roared, "Jelly!" Around them, windows rattled in their frames and slates slid from rooftops, smashing as they hit the ground.

Then the crazed creature from the Black Lagoon licked his rubbery lips, fixed his hungry gaze on the lump of jelly that was Resus's mum, and slithered forward.

"Oh no!" moaned Luke. "Things just got worser!"

Chapter Five
THE BATTLE

"Already told you," said Cleo. "That's not a real word."

"Jeeeellllyyyy!" howled Mr Crudley, as he bore down on the pile of pudding that was Bella Negative.

"OK," agreed Cleo. "It's worser!"

Resus raced towards the monster. "Stop!" he yelled. "Don't you dare eat my mum!"

Luke turned back to Luella. "Tell us what a U.U.S. is, now!" he demanded.

Luella swallowed hard. "It's a Universal Undo Spell," she said. "It's the first spell every trainee witch learns, just in case things go badly wrong."

"I think we're at that stage!" Cleo pointed out. "So, you can do this spell?"

"I think so," croaked Luella.

"You *think* so?"

"Maybe. But if I use, like, one wrong ingredient, the U.U.S. will become a U.U.S.!"

"This is making my head hurt," said Luke. "What in the name of all things hairy are you talking about?"

"I'm worried that I might get the ingredients wrong and change the Universal Undo Spell into an Undo the Universe Spell," said Luella.

"And what does that one do?" Cleo asked.

"It would end the world, sucking us down a black hole of never-ending torment and pain."

"Leave my mum alone!"

Luke sprinted over to where Resus was now wrestling with Mr Crudley, trying to stop the bog monster's ravenous advance towards Bella.

"I've got this, mate!" he cried. "You and Cleo take Luella back to the emporium and get her to make that undo spell!"

As Resus dashed away, Luke rammed his shoulder hard into Mr Crudley's expansive stomach. He bounced back off the big monster's bulbous belly.

"Whoa!"

Concentrating hard, Luke flooded his mind with a cloud of blackness, then sent the sensation searing down towards his feet. His trainers burst as his legs and feet transformed into the lower limbs of his werewolf. The boost of power was enough for him to be able to slide Mr Crudley away from his prey.

Inside the stockroom of Eefa's Emporium, Luella sagged against the side of the cauldron and began to cry. "This is all my fault!" she sobbed.

Cleo lifted the witch's chin. "You can do this!" she insisted.

"Do you think so?" Luella blubbed.

"To be honest, I don't really know," said Cleo with a shrug. "I mean, judging by your previous attempts at spell casting, these are likely to be our final few moments on Earth. But, hey, it's good to stay positive, right?"

"You're right!" cried Luella. "I'm a useless

witch! I never get anything right!"

Resus pulled Cleo gently to one side and took her place. He reached out and took Luella's hand in his. "Are you kidding?" he said kindly. "You're an amazing witch!"

Luella peered up at her dark angel through tear-filled eyes. "How?"

Resus smiled. "You managed to turn half of Scream Street into dessert!" he said. "That's pretty amazing, if you ask me."

"It is?"

"Yes!" said Resus. "So, how about we put our heads together and save the day?"

Luella wiped her eyes with her sleeve and sniffed. "Yeah, all right!" she said, forcing a smile. "Let's do this!"

Wallop!

Mr Crudley barged hard into Luke, knocking him right over the jellified Bella Negative and sending him skidding along the road. With nothing between him and another succulent snack, the bog monster screwed his eyes shut, licked his lips and let out another cry of:

"Jeeellllyyyyy!"

"You stay away from my wife!" commanded a voice.

Mr Crudley opened his eyes to see Alston Negative standing right in front of him. "I will not let you eat Bella. I love her, even if she is a disgusting lump of transparent jelly with eyes and teeth!"

"Blawww!" wobbled Bella. "That's so sweet, honey!"

Wham!

Mr Crudley lashed out with his super-sized stomach and sent Alston flying. Then, mouth wide and salivating, he turned towards the jelly Bella …

… only to be grabbed and wrestled away by a fully formed werewolf.

Long talons tearing the material of Mr Crudley's Hawaiian shirt, the wolf began to drag Mr Crudley away from its best friend's mum.

Luella pressed her hands to the sides of her head and listed ingredients while Resus and Cleo grabbed them from the shelves and dumped them into the waiting cauldron.

"Pencil rubbers!" the young witch cried. "And

… and … oat flakes!"

Resus raced to the far side of the storeroom.

"No, wait!" yelled Luella. "Not oat flakes. *Soap flakes*!"

The vampire spun on the spot. "Are you sure?" he demanded.

"Yes!" exclaimed Luella. "Like, I'm almost positive!"

"We're doomed," said Cleo, calmly. "You know that, don't you Resus?"

"There's still a chance," snapped the vampire. "What next?"

"Water!" Luella instructed. "And lizard tails!"

"Certain?"

"Certain!"

"OK," said Resus, dumping the final ingredients into the mix. "Go for it!"

Luella grabbed her long-handled spoon and began to stir.

"Buuuuurrrpppp!"

The belch was astonishing. Had he not been lost deep inside his werewolf and fighting to protect Bella Negative's life, Luke would have been seriously impressed.

Instead, the wolf found itself surrounded by a swirling brown fog that stung its eyes and drove hot shards of pain up its nose. It staggered backwards, falling to the ground.

Finally, there was nothing to stop Mr Crudley from feasting.

"Jeeeeellllllyyyyyyy!"

The bog monster grabbed the lump of jelly and raised it to his mouth.

Alston was too far away; he could only watch. "Noooooo!"

Luella reached inside the cauldron and pulled out a swirling orb of green and blue.

"Is that it?" Resus asked. "The Universal Undo Spell?"

"Please tell us it is," said Cleo.

"I don't know," Luella admitted. "I've never seen one in real life before, just in textbooks."

Despite the panic, Resus smiled again. "I believe in you," he said.

"I'm glad somebody does!" cried Cleo, diving beneath the table.

Luella kicked open the door to the furnace. "It's been nice knowing you all!" she said. Then she tossed the spherical spell into the roaring fire.

Gleaming white lightning bolts exploded from the chimney above Eefa's Emporium. Crackling with energy, they swept across the sky, striking everyone affected by the love potion and returning life back to normal.

In the graveyard, Mrs Crudley carefully placed Doug's head on the ground and slithered away, whistling, as if nothing had happened. Seconds later, Doug's reassembled body came staggering out from behind a tumbledown crypt.

"Dude," the head beamed. "Are you a sight for sore eyes!"

NoName peered nervously out of the boarded-up window of an abandoned house, breathing a sigh of relief as Eefa staggered around in the garden.

Dixon hit the water of the piranha pond one last time, and decided to stay there while the feisty fish nibbled at his outfit. "It's safer in here," he assured himself.

Dr Skully came to his senses just as he was planting a kiss on Lulu's slavering mouth. He fainted into a disorganized bundle of bones.

And outside Sneer Hall, Bella Negative zapped back to her natural form just as Mr Crudley was about to stuff her down his glutinous gullet. The love spell broken, he gently placed her down on the ground and shuddered.

"I can't believe I nearly ate a vampire!" he said. "Think of the indigestion!"

As the bog monster waddled away, Alston raced over to sweep his wife up into his arms. "I love you, my darling!" he proclaimed, before kissing her passionately.

"Ewww!" said Resus, as he and Cleo stepped out from the emporium to join Luke, who had returned to his normal, human form. "I can't look!"

"Come on, Resus!" said Cleo. "It means the love spell you and Luella created worked after all."

"Yeah," agreed Luke. "In a roundabout, messed up, nearly-destroying-the-universe kind of way!"

That evening, as the moon began to rise, Resus met Luella outside the emporium's stockroom door.

"Well," said the vampire. "That was fun!

Maybe we should, you know, hang out again sometime."

"OMG! I'd love that!" cried Luella. "I mean, if you really want to."

"Yeah, why not?"

"It's just that I think I'm going to be grounded for, like, the next ten years."

The door crashed open and Eefa appeared. She didn't look happy.

"Make that a hundred years, young lady!" she barked, dragging Luella inside.

As the door slammed behind them, Resus pushed his hands deep into his pockets and sauntered away.

Inside the shop, Eefa sighed.

"I admit you did a good job with the Universal Undo Spell," she said. "Thank goodness you got all the ingredients right for once! No nasty side effects."

Luella could only shrug. "Thanks, I think."

"But don't believe for one second that you've gotten away with this, Luella! We'll be having a long chat about the witch's code first thing tomorrow morning!"

With that, Eefa turned and marched towards

the shop door, a long lizard tail sticking out from beneath her dress, swishing from side to side.

"OMG!" hissed Luella. "Lizard *scales*! Not lizard tails!"

Eefa stopped in the doorway. "What was that?"

Luella smiled weakly, and pulled what she hoped was her most honest ever expression.

"Nothing!"

RESUS ROCKS

Chapter One

THE GAME

Thick plumes of mist tumbled through the graveyard, spilling over tombstones like waves crashing onto the rocks of a shoreline. And from the dense fog came the sound of groaning, and shuffling, and the grinding of teeth.

A boy and girl stood in a small clearing between the graves, watching and waiting. They clenched their fists and shifted lightly from foot to foot, ready to pounce as soon as the battle began. Their faces showed no emotion whatsoever.

The first zombie emerged from the mist. Ragged clothes clung to its skeleton-thin frame, which was wrapped in what must once have been human skin. Now it resembled torn leather.

The creature snarled, causing a gush of sticky, scarlet blood to ooze from the missing side of its face. The hole ran from just below its right eye, down through an entirely missing cheek to end at the side of its mouth. Its lips flapped like pieces of wet rubber with every shuffling step.

The undead wretch caught sight of the waiting kids and limped as quickly as it could towards them, just as the rest of the zombie horde emerged from the cascading clouds of mist. Some of them, like the leader of the pack, were almost completely whole. Others had missing limbs, or unseeing eyeballs dangling from veins out of hollow sockets – even exposed sections of brain. But whatever their condition, the entire troop now had the youngsters' scent in their rotting nostrils, and they rushed to attack.

As half-face drew near, the girl leapt into the air, spinning impossibly as wispy tendrils of fog radiated out from her body. Her foot connected with the still-present side of the zombie's face, and the creature's head jerked back. Its decomposing spinal cord snapped with an audible *crack*, and the monster's head was sent flying off to land in the disturbed earth of an anonymous grave.

The zombie sank to its knees. A scream rang out and a digitized number *3,000* appeared, floating above the off-white stump of neck bone. The creature moaned, flickered in and out of view for a second, and then disappeared.

"Yes!" cried a distant voice. "Beat that, Watson!"

As the girl landed lightly, another of the walking dead lunged towards the boy at her side, its mouth open to reveal a severed tongue swarming with maggots. The lifeless beast bore down to bite. The boy stood his ground, then punched straight ahead with his fist, shattering the zombie's ribs. In one swift movement, he grasped the monster's blackened, unbeating heart in his fingers and squeezed until it burst.

Another scream sounded, and a score of *2,000* points appeared as the zombie strobed and vanished.

"What?" exclaimed another disconnected

voice. "That move was worth way more than a measly 2,000 points!"

In the living room of 13 Scream Street, Egyptian mummy Cleo Farr stuck out her tongue at her friend, Luke Watson. "You're just mad because you're being beaten by a girl!"

"That's not true!" said Luke. "I mean, I may be losing to a girl at the moment, but I'll obviously win in the end."

"Is that so?"

"Yes, it is completely so!"

Cleo gripped her game controller and turned back to the high-resolution image on the screen. The rest of the computerized zombies were almost within grabbing distance of the characters.

"Let's do this!" she said, cracking her neck from side to side.

The two friends leapt into action, swinging controllers and pressing buttons to send their on-screen avatars into a fighting frenzy. Before long, zombie body parts were flying through the air.

"That one's yours!" yelled Luke as his character put an end to the rampage of yet another grave escapee. A second drooling creature was waiting behind it, ready to pounce.

"Got it!" hissed Cleo, flicking her thumbsticks in a figure-eight shape. Her character executed a perfect spin kick, decapitating her lifeless attacker.

"Kapow!" she shouted as a score of *4,000* points flashed. "So long, ugly!"

Luke's fists pumped as his character pummelled the next in the advancing horde, earning himself a series of *1,000* points in rapid succession, followed by a bright green *10,000* as his opponent crumbled to dust.

"Bonus!" he cried. "What a game! You've got to love *Zombie Kick Boxer*!"

"Actually, dude… I'm finding it kinda offensive."

Luke turned to the third occupant of the room. Sitting in the armchair behind him and Cleo was a figure with lank hair, rotting skin and a set of yellowing, broken teeth.

"Really, Doug?" asked Luke, surprised. "How can this be offensive?"

"Not all zombies are like that, bro," Doug explained. "Some of us, Yours Truly included, prefer chilling to killing."

"Oh," said Luke, his cheeks flushing red. "I didn't think of it that way. This game was huge back in the normal world and, to be fair, I never thought I'd ever play it in front of an actual zombie. Sorry!"

"No problemo, dude," said Doug with a grin. "It's just that those of us who are, you know, 'not quite dead' never get a good rap in those games."

"I suppose not," said Luke.

"And watching you beat up on my brain-dead bros is dredging up some painful memories from the back of my mind." The zombie paused to scratch at his scalp. "At least, I *think* they're memories. It could just be beetles again."

"Er, a little help over here!" With Luke's character paused, Cleo was having to work harder than ever to defeat the tsunami of rotting corpses as they attacked. Her arms and legs flailed around as she took on the ever-growing tide of breathless biters.

"Whoa!" Luke exclaimed, jumping back into the game as his character disappeared beneath three hungry monsters.

"Hurry!" cried Cleo. "You're— Oh, no!"

It was too late. Luke's lifeline at the top of the screen dropped lower and lower as his pixelated

persona was chomped upon, slashed and gradually torn apart.

The words "GAME OVER" flashed in the centre of the screen.

"Ha!" beamed Doug, jumping to his feet. "You're dead, bro! Hope you come back as a zombie, then you could see this stuff from my perspective. We could totally hang out!"

Luke grinned. "So long as my dad's not around."

"I hear you, wolfy dude," said Doug, making for the living-room door. "Your old man is still a little wary of us grave-dodgers. I get it. I'll catch you on the flip side."

Just as Doug reached out for the handle, the door swung open and Luke's dad strode into the room. At the sight of the zombie, he squealed, dropped his mug of tea and fell against the window frame.

"Sorry, Mr W!" said Doug. "Didn't mean to scare you!"

"Th-that's OK, D-Doug," whimpered Mike Watson from halfway behind the curtain. "I'm still finding the undead a little hard to get used to!" He began to edge around the walking corpse

to his armchair. Then his face paled.

"Yours, I believe," Mike said, plucking a wriggling worm from the back of the chair and handing it over."

"Wilfred!" exclaimed Doug, taking the worm and stuffing it back into his hair as he left the room. "Thanks, man!"

Mike slumped into his chair and tried to calm his breathing.

"You OK, Dad?" Luke asked.

"Never better!" Mike lied. "What are you two kids up to?"

Luke glanced over his shoulder at the zombie carnage on-screen and quickly flicked off his games console. "Not a lot!" he said, smiling. "Why don't you settle back and watch the news while Cleo and I clean up and make you another cup of tea?"

"Well, that sounds very pleasant indeed," said Mike. "Thank you!"

"Any time, Mr Watson!" said Cleo. She switched channels, then picked up the empty mug from the carpet and followed Luke towards the kitchen.

Mike turned his attention to the screen, where

he found himself faced with yet another zombie. This one, however, was merely reading the weather report, so Mike was able to keep his terror in check. At least, a little.

"…and this south-westerly breeze should blow the cursed fog safely away from Scream Street by the end of the week," announced Mitch Flesh, the ragged reporter.

"Thank goodness for that!" said Mike to himself.

The weatherman grinned. "Back to you, Anna!" Then he reached up and tore off his own head, replacing it with that of the female newscaster, Anna Gored.

Mike swallowed hard.

"Thanks Mitch," said the new presenter, snapping her head into place with a loud *click*. "Now, exciting news for music fans. Due to the fog mentioned in the weather report, vehicles are unable to enter or leave Scream Street for the time being. This includes tour buses. As a result, top flesh-metal band Brain Drain have been forced to abandon their tour. They will play the remainder of their concerts here in Scream Street."

Luke and Cleo appeared in the doorway.

"Brain Drain!" cried Luke.

"We've got to tell Resus!" exclaimed Cleo.

The pair raced for the front door, slamming it behind them as they hurried out.

Mike sat silently in his chair for a moment, then said, "Er, hello? What happened to my cup of tea?"

Chapter Two
THE BAND

Resus Negative zipped his skeleton-patterned onesie up to his throat and slumped back against the soft, red lining of his coffin. He was bored. No, more than bored – he was *deathly* bored. There was simply nothing to do.

He had spent some time practising with his vampire cape, the magical cloak handed down to the firstborn in each generation of his family. The cloak gave him access to thousands, if not millions, of items at will, but it also had an unpleasant attitude, and usually gave him the exact opposite of what he needed. Today, he'd tried to produce a tennis racket, but had been handed a tree branch, a roll of bandages and a rather angry cat that had hissed and scratched at him before disappearing through his pet leech's entrance flap.

He'd removed his false fangs (sometimes not being a real vampire had its advantages) and repeatedly flicked them up into the air, seeing if he could get the pointed dentures to stick in the wooden beams above his bed. This had kept him amused for a while – until he missed catching the fangs as they fell and they bit him on the end of his nose.

Now there was nothing to do except lie back and let the world pass him by. But his mum wasn't prepared to let that happen.

"Perhaps you could go for a walk?" Bella Negative suggested on her third trip up to his bedroom in less than an hour. "A bit of fresh air might do you good."

Resus folded his arms across his chest and shuddered. "Fresh air?" he groaned. "Yuck!"

"OK," said Bella, patiently. "Why don't you

practise your guitar?" She gestured towards a gleaming, cherry-red electric six-string sitting in its stand.

Resus sat up and glanced at the instrument, but then slouched back down again. "What's the point?" he demanded. "I'm rubbish!"

Bella scowled. "Stop being so negative all the time!"

"I'm supposed to be negative!" Resus retorted. "My name is Resus Negative!"

Lulu, his pet leech, slithered up the side of her owner's coffin, leaving behind a trail of glistening slime. She stuck out her tongue and gently licked her master's cheek. But Resus just brushed her away.

"Well, you can't stay in bed all day," said Bella, stooping to collect the contents of Resus's washing basket.

"Why not?" her son grumbled. "It's what vampires are supposed to do."

"Now you are deliberately being difficult!" said Bella. "When I was your age—"

Her sentence was interrupted by a knock at the front door.

"I'll be right back," she promised, before

speed-blurring out of the room and arriving in the entrance hallway less than a second later. She opened the door to find Luke and Cleo smiling up at her.

"Hi, Mrs Negative!" beamed Cleo.

"Is Resus in?" asked Luke.

"Yes, he is," replied Bella. "But I'm afraid he's in one of his moods again. Good luck getting him to do anything at all with you today."

Luke and Cleo exchanged a glance, then raced up the stairs. Moments later, Resus came clattering down, fully dressed and grinning from ear to ear, his friends just a few steps behind him.

Bella grabbed Cleo's arm as she made to dash out into the street with the boys. "How did you do that?" she asked, staring after Resus in astonishment. "How did you get him out of his coffin?"

"Simple!" said Cleo. "I just used the magic words – Brain and Drain!"

The queue snaked all the way around Scream Street's central square to a table outside Eefa's Emporium. Seated at the table were three zombies. Individually, they were named Vein, Stix and Dread, but collectively they were Brain

Drain, the world's greatest flesh-metal band.

Vein, the lead vocalist and rhythm guitar player, had formed the band shortly after crawling from his grave several years ago. Like most of the undead, he was unable to remember anything about his former life – the one with a heartbeat. So he took inspiration for his new name from the collection of veins that dangled like spaghetti from an infected, open wound in his chest. He'd often wondered whether this was the injury that had caused his previous life to end. But, whatever had resulted in his demise, he was quite literally eternally grateful, because he couldn't imagine that he had been an idolised rock star before his death.

The first line-up of the band was rather different from the trio now signing albums and posters in Scream Street. Vein had first recruited a bass player named Porridge, who had moved his arms down to his waist to allow his guitar to hang well beneath his knees. There was also a female guitarist called Jazpants. She had stitched three extra fingers onto each of her hands and could play the most incredible solos as a result. With a drummer known as Twonk, Brain Drain set out to conquer the world of zombie music.

Now, years later, Porridge had retired from the band to start a lost-and-found scheme for missing body parts. Jazpants, now with at least fifteen fingers on each hand, was a moderately successful children's book author and could type 15,000 words per minute. Twonk, the drummer, had simply replaced his rotting body parts with new limbs and organs as needed, until there was very little of the original remaining. He eventually changed his name to Stix, and accidentally auditioned to become his own replacement in the group.

Resus hopped nervously from foot to foot as the line moved forward. He was grasping a copy of Brain Drain's latest album, *Spinal Fluid*, eager to get his favourite musicians to sign the cover. Despite Vein's cool looks (the lead singer regularly injected his eyeballs with black ink to give him the appearance of always wearing sunglasses) and Stix's infamous after-show parties, Dread was his favourite. Man, that zombie could play the guitar.

Dr Skully, Scream Street's skeletal schoolteacher, reached the head of the queue. He handed over his copy of *Spinal Fluid*, grateful that his bone-white face wasn't prone to blushing.

"It's, er, for a friend," he said sheepishly. "A friend called D… R… Skully!"

Resus heard someone sigh behind him and turned to discover that one of his classmates was next in line. It was Luella Everwell, niece of the emporium's owner, Eefa.

"Umm… Hey, Resus," said Luella, as casually as she could manage.

"Oh, hi Luella," said Resus, smiling, then turning back to face the front.

"OMG!" Luella whispered to herself. "He made eye contact with me! Stay calm! Stay calm!"

Mr Crudley the bog monster squelched away, and it was Resus's turn. He stepped up to the table. Then he handed his copy of *Spinal Fluid* to Dread and stood, rooted to the spot, grinning like a fool.

The three band members sighed. Another adoring fan shocked into silence by just being in their presence.

"Name!" snapped Dread.

"Um. Sorry. Resus," mumbled the star-struck vampire.

Dread ran his pen over the album cover. "There you go, Um Sorry Resus!"

Resus took the album back and stared at the signature. He couldn't just walk away now! This was his one and only chance to talk to his hero.

"I, er... I play the guitar myself," he said, trying to keep his voice calm.

"Yeah," snarled Dread. "Course you do."

"I do," Resus confirmed. "And I want to be in a band too, one day. I reckon if I practise—"

"Look," barked Dread, interrupting. "Are you buying any more stuff? No? Then move along!"

Blinking hard, Resus turned and shuffled away. But he was still close enough to hear Dread mutter "Loser" as he left.

Luella stepped up to the table, but kept her own copy of the album clutched tightly to her chest. She threw Dread an angry look, then turned to stomp away after Resus.

She found the vampire sitting on the kerb at the back of Eefa's Emporium, his signed album abandoned a few metres away.

"You dropped your album," she said, picking it up.

"I don't want it now," said Resus glumly, gesturing to the phrase "To Um Sorry Resus". "It's ruined."

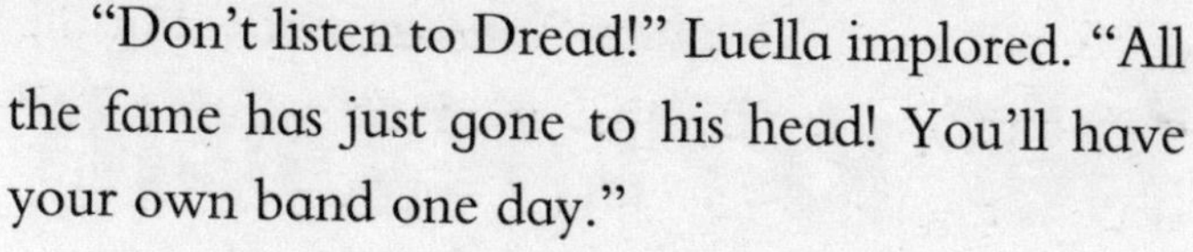

"Don't listen to Dread!" Luella implored. "All the fame has just gone to his head! You'll have your own band one day."

"Yes," said Resus, climbing to his feet. "I will! I can see it now… Resus and the Losers!"

With that, the vampire dropped his album in the gutter again and slunk away.

Luella watched him leave, then spun back towards the Brain Drain signing table. "Nobody insults my dark angel and gets away with it!" she hissed. "I'm going to teach that Dread a lesson he won't forget!"

Chapter Three

THE REPLACEMENT

It was early evening by the time the excitement in the central square had died down. Dread packed his guitar back into its case and set off for Bed Bug Towers, the guesthouse where he and the rest of the band were staying.

He hummed the tune to a new song he was working on as he walked, and tried to fit some lyrics to the melody.

"If I ripped the heart right from your chest,

They'd take me away; cardiac arrest,
So I'll eat you up until you're gone..."

He paused, certain he'd heard footsteps scurrying along the street behind him. But when he turned, there was no one there.

Chuckling to himself, he shook his head. He was imagining things. His skull wobbled a little on the top of his spine.

He went back to his lyrics.

"I'll let your blood flow like a river.
Mop it all up with your juicy liver.
Baby, you're a zombie meal for one!"

There! Dread spun around again. This time he *had* heard someone behind him. But, aside from abandoned roadworks around an open manhole, the street was completely deserted.

The guitarist shook himself, causing his head to jiggle around again. Maybe he'd been working too hard lately. The band had been dashing from the recording studio to gigs, and then to personal appearances. Dread would be happy when he could finally take some time off and get his head down.

That happened sooner than he might have expected.

Stepping up to the front door of Bed Bug Towers, he caught his forehead on the low-hanging "Mind Your Head" sign.

Clang!

The zombie's head was knocked clean off. It crashed to the ground and rolled away.

"Ooof!" cried the decapitated bonce, followed by "Phew, that was close!" as it stopped rolling at the very edge of the open manhole.

Still clutching the guitar case, Dread's body went into overdrive, stomping around, its arms spiralling as it tried to locate the missing head.

"Oi!" shouted the head from the street. "Over here! This way, doofus!"

Without ears to hear, the body simply stumbled around uselessly.

Further down the street, Luella stepped out of the shadows and smiled to herself. She had been sure Dread would notice her following him back to the guesthouse, but she'd managed to dart into doorways and duck behind hedges whenever he looked back.

She spotted the helpless head lying next to the open manhole, and an idea occurred to her. If she could get over to it before Dread's body found it, she would be well on her way to completing Stage One of her cunning and brilliant plan.

Creeping out into view, she tiptoed over to where Dread's separated skull was sitting and stretched out her arm. One short, sharp shove ought to do it.

Before she could push the head into the hole, Dread's body whirled about and began walking in the right direction.

"That's it!" Dread's head directed. "This way! Just be careful you don't— Whoa! Slow down, nitwit! Watch out!"

Luella leapt back just as one of Dread's out-of-control feet kicked its owner in the teeth, sending the head toppling down the open manhole. Then the body blundered on, disappearing into a nearby garden.

Dread's voice echoed from inside the hole. He had landed in a puddle of mud and was left staring up at the circular patch of sky above. "You bumbling idiot!" he yelled at his own body. "When I get out of here, I'm going to kick your

bum! Well, kick my bum! Whatever! You're in deep doo-doo, buddy!"

Checking that the coast was clear, Luella sidled back to the manhole and quickly pulled the metal cover over it, reducing Dread's rants to little more than a distant mumble.

Then she turned and hurried away, trying to look as innocent as possible.

"Hey, this is not funny!" came a muffled cry.

Down in the darkened hole, Dread's nose sniffed at the air. He wasn't alone! He heard a shrill squeak as a sewer rat scurried over to nibble at his cheek, then it scampered beneath the zombie's thick, dreadlocked hair.

"No, stop it!" giggled Dread as the animal's whiskers tickled his skin. "Tee, hee! It's *not* funny, all right? Ha, ha! I'm not laughing! Hee, hee! Pack it in!"

Vein paced the stage and swept the deserted open-air auditorium with his jet-black eyeballs. "Where is he?"

Stix looked up from his drum kit and shrugged. "Dunno, mate," he sniffed.

"We're supposed to be practising that new

song of his, 'Zombie Feasting Time'. How can we do that if he's not here to run us through it?"

"Dunno," said Stix again.

"I knew I should have talked Porridge out of retiring," Vein went on. "We wouldn't have had this nonsense with him, would we?"

Stix frowned for a second as a thought eased its way through what was left of his brain. "Hang on," he said, thinking hard. "I know this one..."

Vein watched his bandmate's face contort as he searched for an answer. But eventually it fell back into its usual blank expression.

"No, I dunno," said Stix.

There was a clatter at the back of the auditorium as someone knocked over an entire row of chairs. The two remaining members of Brain Drain looked up to discover Dread's body tottering towards them, guitar case still clutched in one hand.

"Well, here's *most* of him!" Vein commented.

Ten minutes later, the headless body was on stage with its guitar strung around what remained of its neck.

"Right. Well, we can't do Dread's song until the bit that sings shows up," said Vein. "So, let's

rehearse a new one of mine. Ah-one, two, three, four!"

Stix began banging on the pieces of human skin stretched across his drums. The large percentage of Dread that was present started to strum its guitar.

"When I first met you," Vein sang.

"My eyes popped out.
Literally!
They're still on the floor,
I can't see you no more,
Literally!"

Had any Brain Drain fans been allowed to listen to the rehearsal, they might have commented that, while the gory flesh-metal lyrics were the perfect accompaniment to Stix's driving beat, the song was ruined when Dread's body fell off the front of the stage and its guitar snapped in half with an almighty *twang!*

"Stop, stop!" yelled Vein. "This is useless. We're just going to have to cancel the rest of the gigs."

"Perhaps not!" squeaked a small voice.

Vein and Stix both jumped as Luella appeared behind them on the stage.

"What do you mean?" the lead singer demanded.

"OK," said Luella, taking a deep breath. "It's-just-that-I-know-this-really-great-guy-who's-brilliant-on-the-guitar-and-he-knows-all-your-songs-and-plays-them-all-the-time-'cause-he's-such-a-big-fan-and-he-probably-knows-them-all-backwards-although-that-probably-wouldn't-be-much-help-really-would-it? Well-anyway-he-looks-great-and-he-dresses-really-cool-and-I-think-he-could-be-amazing-if-you-give-him-the-chance-to-be-in-your-band-with-you!"

Vein glanced down at Dread's body as it tried to untangle itself from a knot of microphone leads and twisted guitar strings. A thin smile spread across his green, chiselled features.

"Let's talk, little lady."

"Brain Drain! Brain Drain! Brain Drain!"

Resus paced up and down backstage as the audience continued to cheer for their favourite band.

"I can't do this!" he said, sliding his guitar off and heading for the exit.

Luella grabbed him by the arm. "Oh yes, you can!" she said. "I haven't put all this work in for you to quit at the last minute!"

Resus peered at her. "What work?"

Luella shrugged, slipping back into what she hoped was her innocent face. "You know, just like, err … going up to Vein and suggesting that he audition you to be Dread's replacement."

"*Temporary* replacement," Resus reminded her. "Someone could find his head at any minute."

"Oh, I don't think that's very likely."

"What? Why not?"

"No reason! Now, just relax, my dark angel. You'll be great!" She hung the vampire's guitar around his neck again. "You did really well in the audition."

"That was different!" Resus scoffed. "There weren't a hundred screaming audience members out there then."

"More like four hundred, actually," Luella corrected. "The place is packed!"

Resus took his guitar off again. "That's it, I'm out of here!"

Luella dragged him back. "Not a chance!"

Resus smiled weakly. "But, what if I let the band down?"

Luella grabbed the vampire by the shoulders and looked straight into his eyes. "You absolutely won't, because you're brilliant and I totally believe in you."

Before Resus could reply, Vein appeared in the wings and slapped him on the back. "Come on, buddy," he said. "You're up!" Then he and Stix strode onto the stage to rapturous applause.

As Luella handed him his guitar, Resus paled beneath his already pasty face paint. "I think I'm going to be sick!" he gulped.

Chapter Four

THE EGO

Resus leapt down the four steps from the stage into the wings, the cheers from the crowd still echoing in his ears. He spotted Luella and raced over to hug her tightly.

"That was *sick*!" he cried.

"OMG!" gasped Luella to herself. "A hug! A real hug! Keep it together! Remember to breathe!"

Resus released the young witch from his grasp and danced around happily. "Did you hear my solo in 'Earworm'?" he exclaimed.

"I heard it!"

"The crowd went crazy!"

"I know! It was brilliant!"

"And the twiddly bit I did at the end of 'Coffin Crazy!' And the way I added the down-string jabs in 'Lung Blaster!' Vein looked over and winked right at me!"

"Wicked!"

"At least, I think he winked at me. It might have been the dye shifting around inside his eyeball. But he definitely seemed pleased with what I was doing."

Luella beamed and opened her arms for another hug. "I'm so happy for you, Resus. I thought we might—"

Before she could finish, Vein and Stix appeared from the stage and made for their dressing room. Resus left Luella and ran over to join them.

"Hey guys, wait up!" he called. "I've got some song ideas I want to talk over with you."

Luella watched in silence as they disappeared.

Luke and Cleo sat at a table in Eefa's, tucking into one of her trademark Banshee Burgers

– three patties of meat with extra cheese, onion slices and lashings of extra-hot homemade chilli sauce.

Cleo watched in disgust as Luke tore into his burger, spraying bits of food everywhere. "You know, back when we were alive, my dad and I had an official food taster," she said.

"Yeah?" asked Luke through a mouthful of onion.

"It's true," continued Cleo. "It was his job to take a bite of everything our servants brought to us at the dinner table, just in case someone was plotting to poison the great Pharaoh or his precious daughter."

"Imagine," said Luke, barely listening. He paused in demolishing his burger just long enough to stuff a fistful of ketchup-coated chips between his teeth.

"I'm really glad we didn't hire someone like you for the job," said Cleo.

"I'll bet," said Luke. Then he looked up. "Hang on... Why?"

"Because there wouldn't be any food left by the time you'd finished! I hate to think how you eat when you're a werewolf!"

Luke leaned across the table and pulled a scary face. "Want to make me angry and find out?" he growled. But he couldn't keep the expression in place, and soon both he and Cleo were giggling.

The bench shook as Resus dropped into the seat beside the mummy.

"Oh, look!" exclaimed Luke, bowing his head. "The rock star's here!"

"Not just a rock star," added Cleo, "a rock star in our favourite band!"

"And he's lowering himself to spend time with us!" said Luke. "We are honoured!"

"I think I might faint, actually!" said Cleo.

"I'm not surprised!" said Luke. "It's not often you get to spend time in the presence of a musical legend."

Cleo faked a *gasp* as an idea occurred to her. "You should totally get his autograph!"

"I will!" said Luke. "Excuse me, Mr Negative, but would you mind signing..." He jumped up in his seat and spun round. "My bum?"

"Yeah, yeah!" Resus chuckled as Luke sat down and high-fived Cleo. "But, whatever you say, it *is* pretty cool, isn't it?"

"Only completely!" agreed the mummy.

"We asked Eefa to keep an extra Banshee Burger warm for you," said Luke. "You've got to tell us everything!"

"Yeah," said Cleo. "What's Vein really like? Does he do that swaggery walk in real life, or is it just on stage?"

"Actually, I've only popped in to say that I can't come out tonight," said Resus. "I'm working on some new stuff with the other two. Laters!"

Then he jumped up and hurried for the door. His friends watched him go, mouths open.

"Seriously?" asked Luke.

"I thought *we* were the other two!" exclaimed Cleo.

As Resus reached the main entrance to the emporium, the bat above the door let out a shrill *squeak* and Luella entered.

"OMG!" she cried. "Resus, I nearly bumped right into you! Hey, perhaps we—"

"Not now, Luella," said Resus, striding past her. "I'm in a hurry."

The bat above the door watched impassively as the witch bit her lip and blinked back tears.

"I've got a hunger,
Welling up inside,
It's like an illness,
Eating me alive."

Vein's powerful voice screeched through the sound system, sending the dials on the band's soundboard flicking up to the maximum level of 13. Operating the system was a heavily tattooed ogre named Spider. He reached out and gently adjusted the dials to subtly lower the volume of the singer's microphone. Then he pushed up the slider connected to Resus's electric guitar as he carried out his solo.

"I've got this craving.
I feel it in my core,
I'll stop at nothing,
I want it more and more."

The audience, a vast mob consisting mainly of zombies, cheered. Those who had managed to retain both their legs danced wildly in front of the stage, while anyone with matching arms played air guitar along with the newest member of the band.

"I need fame,
Chant my name,
Look at me,
What do you see?"

After the group's third gig, Resus had pulled a pair of black sunglasses from inside his cloak and now he kept them on while he was playing. He hammered at the strings of his guitar, stepping forward from the rear of the stage when it was time to play his solos.

"I need fame,
Chant my name,
Feels so good,
Knew it would!"

Before long, Spider had given him his own microphone so that he could join in with the backing vocals. The ogre continued to boost the volume of the vampire's instrument and lower

Vein's mic whenever he got the chance.

"Get a taste for fame,
Old friends you will shun,
Goes straight to your head,
If you've still got one."

Dread's headless body continued to wander aimlessly around Scream Street over the next few days. Luke and Cleo tried to capture it to help it rest, but anyone who went near the clumsy corpse was likely to get an elbow in the eye for their trouble.

The pair couldn't get near Resus, either – even when they spotted him walking to or from Eefa's Emporium with his arms around his bandmate's shoulders. Luke had tried to stop and chat on one such occasion, but Spider had quickly stepped in to insist that autographs would only be given at the end of that night's concert.

"Fame is here today,
And gone tomorrow,
First so much joy,
Then so much sorrow."

By the end of the week, posters announcing that Brain Drain were to play extra concerts in Scream Street began to appear. Only now the band's name had been changed to "Brain Drain, featuring Resus Negative".

Luke caught Luella standing and staring at one of the posters. "Hey," he said kindly. "Are you OK?"

Luella looked up at him through wet eyes, then turned and ran off.

Luke frowned. "This has gone far enough!" he growled, and he strode towards the concert arena. Dodging Spider, he managed to get back-stage and found Resus's dressing room. It wasn't difficult: the door had a big gold star with the vampire's name printed in the centre. Lulu the leech was whimpering outside.

Luke raised his fist to knock, but the door opened out suddenly, sending both Luke and Lulu sprawling. Resus charged out of the dress-ing room, his guitar slung over his shoulder. He didn't look back.

Luella watched Luke stride past angrily, an

unhappy leech tucked beneath his arm. She glanced up at the Brain Drain flag fluttering over the stage and scowled.

"How dare he ignore me?" she spat. "Without me, he's nobody! Nobody! Well, he can wave goodbye to his precious concerts."

Closing her eyes, she began to wave her hands around in the air.

"Twisting, turning, seven winds blow,
Feel the wrath of my tornado!"

For a second, nothing happened. Then the wind picked up speed and changed direction. The Brain Drain flag flicked from one side of the flag-pole to the other, then began flapping madly as Vein, Resus and Stix walked onstage below. The audience, almost all zombies again, screamed, cheered and tossed body parts into the air at the sight of the flesh-metal stars.

Luella smiled wickedly and rubbed her hands together. "Well, that spell was just a breeze!" she cackled.

Chapter Five
THE FOG

Vein's voice echoed out across Scream Street.

"I've got an earworm,
It's eating on my brain,
I've got an earworm,
It's driving me insane!"

Still lying in the mud at the bottom of the sealed manhole, Dread's head twitched back and forth in time to the distant music.

"Oh, man, this one's my favourite!" he commented to the sewer rat as it reappeared from one of the side tunnels. "Vein and I wrote this song together during my first week in the band."

The head sniffed, and so did the rat.

"Oh, ah..." said Dread's head. "My nose itches! Hey, Dennis, do you think you could...?"

The rat scurried forward and rested its front paws on Dread's leathery cheek, then it scratched the zombie's nose with its teeth.

"Oh, yeah!" said Dread. "That's it! Just there!"

He blinked as a dense green fog began to blow through the holes in the metal cover above, slowly filling up the underground space.

"Oh, dear," said the head. "I don't like the look of this."

Dread growled as his eyes glazed over. Then he snatched out with his blistered, pus-filled lips and swallowed the rat whole.

It re-emerged unharmed from his severed throat moments later.

✻

The entire zombie audience whooped as Resus raced from one side of the stage to the other, dropping to his knees halfway and sliding the rest. The raised latch of a wooden trapdoor in the stage tore the material of his trousers, but the vampire was far too engrossed in his music to either notice or care.

He flopped onto his back in front of Stix's drum kit and performed an impromptu solo. This had to be the best day of his entire— He paused his thought midway. Something was different.

Thick emerald-coloured gas flooded the floor of the stage, causing Resus to jump back to his feet. He looked around as the fog spilled off the front of the raised platform and into the wildly dancing audience.

"Wow!" he cried over the sound of the music. "These effects just get better and better!"

"What effects?" demanded Stix.

"I'm loving the smoke machine!" bellowed Resus. "It's fang-tastic!"

Stix's hairy eyebrows knitted together. "We haven't got a smoke machine!" he shouted back.

"Ours was confiscated when we played the Dragon Stadium in Beijing. It made everyone think the giant ornamental egg was hatching!"

Resus blinked. "So, if this isn't from a smoke machine— Hey!" He yelled as one of the zombies at the front of the audience reached up onto the stage and grabbed his ankle tightly. "Autographs later, buddy!"

But as Resus kicked the zombie away, another made a lunge for him. Then another, and another…

"Whoa!" cried Resus, backing up to where Vein was singing. "What's going on with that lot?"

Vein didn't respond. Instead, he dropped his microphone and wrapped his hands around Resus's neck.

"I've got an earworrrrrrr!" raged the singer. "Grrrooaaarrr!"

"Vein!" croaked Resus, his fingers finally leaving the strings of his guitar as he tried to pull the singer's hands away from his throat. "What's wrong, man?"

Vein snapped his teeth together as he pushed towards Resus's face. The vampire pulled away,

only to hear a horrifying wail from behind. He spun to see Stix clambering over his drum kit, an expression of crazed hunger etched over his features.

Resus didn't understand exactly what was going on, but he knew he had to get away. He turned towards the audience, hoping to leap off the stage and push his way through the crowd, but the green fog had affected every zombie out there, too. At the back of the auditorium, Spider was using a folded chair to fend off his own attackers.

Turning to try to force his way past Vein and into the wings, Resus suddenly noticed the trapdoor. Dropping to his knees, he slid back the metal bolt and lifted the escape hatch. He tossed his guitar down first and, with a final glance back at the rioting undead, dove head first into the darkness below.

Outside the venue, people ran screaming as zombies lurched after them in the green fog. He heard a mournful moan at his left and swung out with his guitar, catching a ravenous monster in the face – *twang!* – and sending the zombie's head spinning away into a nearby garden.

Then Resus dropped his guitar and ran for his life.

He was sprinting so fast that he didn't see Luella standing in the centre of the square, wringing her hands together again, this time with worry.

"Oh, broomsticks!" she wailed. "This does not look good! OK, Luella, you can fix this. You've *got* to fix this!"

The young witch waved her hands through the ever-thickening fog and chanted. "Weather spell gone horribly wrong! Fog begone, begone, begone!"

A twinkling rainbow rose up above the chaos.

"I've got this," Luella said to herself. She waved her hands again. "Seven winds I summon thee. Blow this fog back out to sea!"

This time, a small black thundercloud appeared directly over her. A bolt of lightning *zzzapped* out of it and hit her on the head.

"Ow!"

Resus ran as fast as his patent leather dress shoes would let him. There was a veritable horde of zombies on his tail. Skidding on the pavement, he turned into a side street … and froze. It was a dead end.

By the time he turned around, the undead throng was almost upon him, teeth bared.

Resus backed up against the far wall. "No, no, no!" he cried. "This isn't happening!"

The zombies lurched ever closer. The vampire could smell the rancid odour of decomposing flesh.

"Please go away!" he begged, terrified. "It's not fair! There's only one of me!"

"Let's make that two, shall we?" said Cleo, landing cat-like beside him.

Luke dropped heavily to the ground on the vampire's other side, his hands already transformed into those of his inner werewolf. "More like three!" he grunted. "But I've really got to work on my landings!"

"Guys!" cried Resus. "I've never been happier to see you!"

"You're a total troll, Resus Negative!" barked Cleo. "But we're still here for you."

"Friends forever," said Luke. "Whatever!"

The trio adopted fighting poses.

Cleo cricked her neck from side to side. "Let's

do this thing!"

The battle erupted and, within a few moments, zombie body parts were flying left, right and centre.

"The problem with being famous," shouted Luke, as he grabbed Vein by the arms and ripped them off at the shoulder, "is that everybody wants a piece of you!"

A zombie hissed in Luke's ear, its few remaining teeth gnashing together. Luke spun and kicked it hard in the chest, sending the creature crashing to the ground.

"Bonus!" he shouted.

The boys ducked as Cleo shot over their heads, knocking off a head with her foot, using her fists to take out another.

"Double bonus!" The mummy grinned as she landed.

Resus was focussed on Doug. The usually chilled zombie's eyes were flashing with untempered rage. The vampire placed his hands on Luke and Cleo's shoulders, then flicked both feet into the air. His shoes connected with Doug's jaw, sending his head rocketing high up into the air.

"Triple bonus!" Resus shouted. Then he turned to the twitching, headless figure at his feet and added, "Sorry, Doug!"

Lightning struck Luella again and again as she threw her head back and screamed to the sky.

"Day is night, and night is day!
Blow the wind the other way!"

The Brain Drain flag above the stage flipped to fly in the opposite direction.

"Yes!" cried Luella, as the green fog began to disperse. "A spell that works! At least, I think it does."

The fog cleared from the side street to reveal a vast pile of dismembered, groaning zombies – and three figures striking heroic poses among them.

"Game over!" said Luke.

"No lives lost!" Cleo added.

"Thanks to you guys," Resus pointed out.

There was a whizzing sound, and then Doug's head landed hard on the concrete. "Ow!" he groaned, eyes flicking up to the trio. "What happened here, dudes?"

"You don't remember?" Resus asked.

"Not a thing, vampire bro," Doug replied.

"Then nothing happened," said Resus with a smile. "Nothing at all!"

The vampire led his friends through the corpse-filled carnage, pausing when he found his fellow members of Brain Drain slumped against a garden gate.

"Whoa!" moaned Vein. "That must have been a big night!"

"Yeah!" agreed Stix. "I'm still legless!"

As Cleo and Luke retrieved the musicians' missing limbs, Resus stooped to chat with them. "Guys, I'm leaving the band."

"Why?" demanded Stix.

"Creative differences," replied Resus. "You wanted to eat me, and I didn't want to be dinner."

"Oh."

"You can't leave yet," said Vein. "We still haven't found Dread's head."

"Er, I think I might be able to help you there," said Luella, stepping into view.

"I've got an earworm,
It's eating on my brain,
I've got an earworm,
It's driving me insane."

The first gig performed by the newly reunited Brain Drain attracted a record crowd. Dread, head now firmly reattached to his shoulders, stepped forward to execute a complex guitar solo.

Dr Skully stood near the front of the crowd, his bony fingers clapping happily in time to the music, until he spotted Mr Crudley nearby. Then he thrust them deep into his pockets.

"I'm only here for a friend," he whimpered.

"I've got an earworm,
It's eating all the rot."

Further back in the crowd, Resus pushed his way through the now much friendlier audience of zombies to reach Luke and Cleo.

"Luella can't come out," he shouted, trying to be heard over the music. "Eefa's grounded her

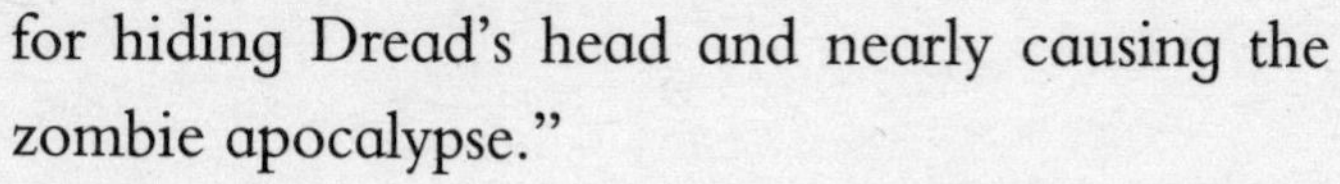

for hiding Dread's head and nearly causing the zombie apocalypse."

"Shame!" hollered Cleo. "This is a great song!"

"Yeah, the band's not bad!" said Luke with a wink, as he and Cleo both produced a pair of sunglasses and slipped them on.

"It would be better if we were in it!" said the mummy.

Laughing, Resus slipped on his own pair of shades. Then he wrapped his arms around his friends' shoulders and the trio joined in with the lyrics of their favourite band.

"I've got an earworm.
Does it hurt? Yes, a lot!"

AN EXCERPT FROM THE NEW BOOK IN THE SERIES

Chapter One

THE HOUSE

The werewolf's powerful legs pounded as Luke picked up speed. Large feet covered with thick fur stomped down the dense, decaying vegetation that covered the woodland floor. Ah, there was nothing like taking his werewolf legs out for a run! With every stride, dead trees shot past in an impossible blur.

Ahead lay a river. Just an innocent, slow-moving body of water at first glance, but Luke knew it contained fish that could strip flesh from bone in seconds with their razor-sharp teeth. Anyone - or anything - foolish enough to dip a toe into the ice-cold stream would instantly pay the price.

When he reached the bank, Luke used all the power of his werewolf legs to leap into the air. He stretched his arms towards a thick branch over-hanging the river, managing somehow to grip the black, rotting wood and using his momentum to carry himself forward. Luke prayed the branch would hold... And it did.

He landed hard on the far side of the river, one furry heel splashing into the water's edge and causing a flurry of activity as its deadly occupants fought for a taste of flesh. But by the time the fish reached the bank, fangs snapping, the potential meal was already gone.

Just one obstacle left – the enormous fallen tree that had outwitted Luke on more than one early morning workout. Today, however, the run was not going to end here. Today, he would continue on, deeper into the unexplored part of the woods.

Timing each stride carefully, Luke jumped as he reached the immovable tree trunk, both feet landing squarely on the rough bark. His werewolf knees took over, bending into a crouch then – muscles screaming with the effort – propelling him up into the air and over into a perfect somersault.

This time, he would land safely. This time, the run would continue.

"Yes!"

Then he skidded and slammed, face first, into a solid brick wall and fell to the ground with an embarrassing *crump*!

"Ow!" cried Luke Watson, rubbing his nose

as his partial werewolf transformation began to reverse. He pulled his fingers away and saw they were smudged with blood.

Untangling his now human legs, he climbed to his feet and examined the wall that had stopped him in its tracks. He ran his hand over the peeling purple paint, feeling the rough brickwork underneath.

"Who on earth put this house here?" he asked out loud.

Mike Watson opened the oven and grinned as the aroma of roasting chicken wafted towards him. Memories of life before Scream Street came flooding back: Sunday dinner with music playing in the background – a proper vinyl record, of course. Then a quick snooze in front of the TV while his wife did the dishes and Luke finished his homework.

Today was going to be a good day!

"Mmm! Delicious!" he declared, sliding the chicken from the oven shelf and carrying it to the dining table to sit beside a mound of roast potatoes and a bowl of steaming vegetables.

Sue, his wife, joined him at the table, opening a bottle of ice-cold lemonade.

No, strike that, Mike thought. Today was going to be a *great* day!

He had just picked up the carving knife and was holding it above the roast when Luke skidded to a stop in the doorway. He was out of breath, and wiping his still-bloody fingers on the back of his jeans.

"Mum! Dad!" he cried. "They've put up another house in the woods! Must be new arrivals. Can I go over to say hello?"

"Of course," said his mum, sliding the cork back into the lemonade bottle before she had poured a single drop. "We should all go."

Mike sat down heavily at the table, his dream of a great day already starting to unravel. "No, no, no!" he cried, waving his hands. "I have no desire whatsoever to find out what manner of monster has moved in down the road."

He took the bottle of lemonade from his wife and pulled out the cork again.

"I am about to tuck into a nice, ordinary Sunday lunch. Please just let me enjoy it."

Silence fell over the dining room.

Mike sighed happily. He'd done it. He'd stood his ground and won. Today wasn't going to be about mad monsters and crazy creatures. Today was going to be about normal things, things like lemonade, steaming carrots and roast chicken.

Reaching out, he pulled a leg from the cooked bird in the centre of the table and held it under his nose, taking a long sniff. This was going to be the best meal he'd had in—

Suddenly, the roast chicken jumped up to stand in its serving tray and glare at him. No, thought Mike. That can't be right! The chicken hasn't got a face! How can it be glaring at me?

Before Mike could continue with this train of thought, the chicken lunged forward and snatched its recently detached leg from his grip. Then it turned, leapt down from the dinner table, and hopped out the door.

The Watson family watched it leave in silence. Then, as they heard the front door slam, Luke turned back to his parents and shrugged.

"Looks like the chicken's off," he said.

Mike clamped a hand over his mouth and dashed for the bathroom.

Thirty minutes later, Luke was standing outside the new house in the woods with Resus

Negative and Cleo Farr. Since his family had moved to Scream Street, Luke had taken part in numerous adventures with his new friends – adventures that had seen the vampire and Egyptian mummy come to his rescue just as many times as he'd been there for them. Now the trio was inseparable, especially on days like today, when there was somewhere new and exciting to explore.

"See!" said Luke. "It looks like a normal, old haunted house."

"And you reckon it just appeared out of nowhere?" asked Cleo.

"Well, it wasn't here yesterday," said Luke. "I've gone running in the woods every day for weeks. I would have noticed if there'd been a great big house in the way."

Resus stepped back to take in the front of the house all at once. "I've never heard of an entire house just appearing overnight before."

Luke shrugged. "Maybe it was an emergency relocation for someone by G.H.O.U.L.?" The Movers from the Government Housing of Unusual Lifeforms (G.H.O.U.L.) had relocated Luke's own family to Scream Street when his werewolf identity became known.

"So, who do you think lives here?" asked Resus.

"Hmmm," mused Cleo. "It's not fancy enough to be vampires. Not gross enough to be bogey-men. And not stinky enough to be werewolves."

Luke spun to face her. "Oi!"

Cleo stuck out her tongue, then thrust her hands onto her hips. "You think we don't know you've been out running with those werewolf legs?" she demanded. "You pass my house on your way home – and let me tell you, sweat really sticks to werewolf fur!"

TO BE CONTINUED...